David L. Ulin

LABYRINTH

David L. Ulin is the author of *The Lost Art of Reading: Why Books Matter in a Distracted Time* and *The Myth of Solid Ground: Earthquakes, Prediction, and the Fault Line Between Reason and Faith*. He is also the editor of three anthologies: *Cape Cod Noir, Another City: Writing from Los Angeles*, and *Writing Los Angeles: A Literary Anthology*, which won a 2002 California Book Award. Ulin is book critic of the *Los Angeles Times*.

First published by GemmaMedia in 2012.

GemmaMedia
230 Commercial Street
Boston, MA 02109 USA

www.gemmamedia.com

© 2012 by David L. Ulin

Printed in the United States of America

978-1-936846-08-5

Library of Congress Cataloging-in-Publication Data

Ulin, David L.
    Labyrinth / David L. Ulin.
        p. cm. — (Gemma open door)
    ISBN 978-1-936846-08-5
    1. Middle-aged men—Fiction. 2. Self-realization—Fiction.
3. San Francisco (Calif.)—Fiction. I. Title.
    PS3621.L438L33 2012
    813'.6—dc23

                                        2012040237

Cover by Night & Day Design

Inspired by the Irish series of books designed for adult literacy, Gemma Open Door Foundation provides fresh stories, new ideas, and essential resources for young people and adults as they embrace the power of reading and the written word.

Brian Bouldrey
North American Series Editor

GEMMA

Open Door

ONE

On a Plain

He was thinking, as the waters of the Bay rose up outside the airplane window in those last moments before the landing gear touched the tarmac, of a scene he had witnessed through another window a few months before. It was a garden party. The Sunday afternoon, warm in Los Angeles, was one of those dry November days that shimmer up like mirages. The air was sere and desert dusky, the light as thin and hollow as a watercolor wash. He had been drinking a beer in the kitchen and talking to someone, he couldn't remember, when he noticed Annie's friend Sylvie pushing her six-year-old son on a swing set in the yard. Sylvie would push and the kid would giggle, and then she'd spread her arms in an exaggerated X, like a scarecrow in a field.

Sylvie was thin like that, just sticks and skin. Her face was a collage of protuberances arranged beneath a crown of lank brown hair. Through the window, he could see her clenched fists, the tilt of her head, the forward angle of her hips. If he'd been outside, he knew, he would be able to hear her, a little bit frantic and excited at once. Sylvie had just had a double mastectomy. Over the summer, she'd been diagnosed with a particularly fast moving breast cancer, and was now, as the saying goes, *fighting for her life*.

The first time he'd ever heard that

phrase, he'd been six himself, driving around Long Beach with his father on the morning after Robert Kennedy was shot. *Senator Kennedy is fighting for his life*, the radio kept saying. He'd imagined the wounded man lying on a stretcher, fists balled and swinging, as if he were duking it out with death. Thinking about that, he glanced again at Sylvie's hands, so small and bony they looked like walnuts. They didn't appear strong enough to battle their way through the fading autumn light.

And yet, this was precisely what Sylvie was doing, fighting the good fight, standing up for as long as she could. She was out in the yard, with her kid, really *with* him, as if whatever connection she might make here would leave a

trace that would linger, for a while anyway, after she was gone. Annie hated it
when he thought that outcomes were
inevitable. But what Annie didn't understand was that he didn't begrudge the
battle: not Sylvie's or anyone's. That it
was futile only made it more necessary
to *be here now*.

It was a lesson he was trying to learn
also: to find a way to get clear of all the
noise. Maybe, if you could fully inhabit
one moment, all that other stuff would
fade, leaving only the paleness of the
sunlight and the image of a mother and
a son, in the instant before time betrayed
them, playing together in the yard.

The plane touched down with a series
of skidding bumps. The brakes kicked in

and he was pushed forward in his seat. Outside forces, all these outside forces. The older he got, the more he felt . . . *buffeted* the word was, as if he himself were caught in turbulence, tossed from side to side. He didn't know why Sylvie had come into his mind. He was not dying (except, of course, in the way that we are all dying), and it had been years since he had pushed a child on a swing. Yet he could feel the betrayal, that time was not his friend any longer. (Another illusion: that it had ever been.)

His restlessness was intensified by the proximity of San Francisco, towers glittering across the Bay. It had been his first city, and its streets were a labyrinth of memory. He had lived here the year after high school, and the experience still rose up to remind him of . . . what? His long-lost possibilities? No, although possibility was part of it. He had been eighteen, on his own for the first time, living in a studio apartment in the Haight. All along, he'd known he would not be staying. When the year was up, he would go to college, and yet, this only had heightened the effect of a ticking clock. He remembered taking the Number 7 bus up Market Street, memorizing the storefronts, buildings stark against the sky like jagged teeth. Before or since, he'd never paid such attention to anything. Thirty years later, he could still be stopped by the right cast of white Pacific light, the scent of eucalyptus, the angle of a terra cotta doorway. All those details and sensations, sense memories of the city, in which the moment was equally present and always, always out of reach.

Finally, the plane pulled up to the gate and cut its engines, and he made his way into the Oakland airport. He was here for the night: an afternoon meeting and then back home tomorrow. He texted Annie to let her know he'd arrived. It was late morning, and in Los Angeles, she was at work, teaching toddlers in the library until it was time to get Sadie at school. Jonah would come home later on the city bus. His son was a high school student already, big and bearded, not so much younger than he himself had been when he'd come to the Bay Area. He stepped onto the sidewalk, momentarily stilled by the crisp clarity of the air.

It felt *redolent*, but the more he tried to think of what, the more it eluded him. It was like memory—attempt to pin it down and it slipped from your grasp. The only way to deal with memory was sidelong, in a series of glances.

TWO

city City CITY

Yes . . . redolent. He could feel the past as he walked up Powell Street from the BART station, bag across his shoulder like a sling. He was looking for the easiest way to navigate Nob Hill. There was no good option, so he took a left on Post and went to Taylor, where he humped a ragged passage up the slope. The hotel was on Taylor and California, cattycorner from Grace Cathedral, which squatted, gray-white and hulking, like a model built for God. He loved the Cathedral and its stolid air of reassurance. He couldn't help drawing solace from it, as if, were you to believe in something hard enough, you might make it true.

The first time he'd set foot inside had been when he lived here, to attend services with his friends Jack and Brooke after a July 4th car wreck on Highway 101. Even then, it had seemed strange, since none of them were believers. Their faith was in an invented mix of magical thinking and serendipity. He could never see the Cathedral without thinking of that moment, the three of them so young. Brooke wore a skirt. He and Jack were in clean jeans and collared shirts, sighing in relief that they were here at all. If he had thought about it, he would have understood how out-of-place he was. But then, that had been the point: to break with the expected, to step outside the narrative, to create not the world that had been imagined for him but the one he had imagined for himself.

And yet, what was this world he had imagined? He couldn't say. He hadn't come here to make a real break, but instead to *take a break*. Maybe this was why that time tugged at him—not because of what it said about his possibilities, but because the whole thing had been an illusion, a story he liked to tell himself. He could see how he looked at eighteen, long-haired, wearing a Guatemalan pullover, the same kind Jonah now wore when he went to Venice Beach with his high school friends. He remembered wandering the streets of San Francisco like a mendicant, through all those endless loops and meandering spirals. Maybe what had made it so intense had been his understanding that it was temporary, that here, for a year anyway, *time had stopped*. Maybe that was why he had paid attention, because he had known all along that it wasn't going to last. Briefly, the image of Sylvie, out in the yard with her six-year-old, flickered across the inside of his eyes. *Be here now*, he found himself thinking. *Be here now*.

There it was, he thought, as he turned into the lobby of the hotel, up the short flight of marble steps, one, two, three, to the reception desk. The central irony of his adult life was that of all the ideas he had ever tried on, the whole thing turned on . . . Ram Dass? Even as a teenager, he'd never taken him seriously. Yet, here he was, murmuring his most famous phrase as it were a mantra. *Strange*, he thought, *strange what sticks and strange what doesn't*, as he got directions to his room.

Upstairs, he threw his bag on the bed and opened the shades, looked out at the city spread before him in a tableau. His window faced east, towards the Embarcadero—although he couldn't see it. He could barely glimpse a sliver of the Bay Bridge, angling beyond the foot of California Street like an iron web. He watched a cable car chuff up the hill, stopping next to the Fairmount, tourists climbing on and off like animated figures in their multi-colored clothes. Nothing seemed quite real, as if seeing the city from a distance left him at an unbridgeable remove. He stood at the window for a long moment, trying to imagine his way into the scene. It would have been nothing to go downstairs, walk into the brilliant noontime, and yet he couldn't bring himself to move. Instead, he turned and unpacked his laptop, tapped into the wireless network of the hotel. *Another window*, he thought, *another kind of window*, as he checked his email, confirming his meeting, the time and place. It was a formality, this meeting, a loose face-to-face without much at stake. It was the sort of thing that could have been done over Skype or even the telephone, except for the vague factor of good will. But that was okay. He was happy to be in San Francisco— or, at least, he thought he was.

THREE

Secret History

The truth was, he was in San Francisco in pursuit of history, a secret history kick-started on Facebook. He had joined with the belief that it would let him keep watch over his children, who seemed to live within its pages, wandering the endless weave of cyberspace as he'd once walked this city's streets. He watched Jonah and Sadie from a distance, *lurking*, a word that caught the flavor of it precisely, as if he were looking around the side of a virtual wall. Then the friend requests drifted in: colleagues and co-workers, other parents, serendipitous contacts, and, at last, a slow trickle of old friends.

The first contacts were oddly thrilling, like postcards from another world. He would log on and, boom, there were images, smaller than stamps, of people he had known in high school, features tauter, slacker, more deeply rendered by the effects of time. He routinely accepted the requests, even when he didn't care about the person. And here was another secret, that he almost never cared, that it almost never mattered to him who showed up, since it was more the *act* of materializing that intrigued him, the insistence of these echoes to assert themselves. He'd read how Facebook was effacing memory, enabling the past to infect the present, with consequences that we couldn't know. How could we move on if everyone we'd ever met was all of a sudden able to find us? How could we re-invent ourselves? He wasn't sure about that. The fact that someone existed as a name and photograph didn't mean much, especially if you didn't interact with them. And anyway they were almost always from the wrong people. They weren't Brooke or Jack, with whom he'd kept in touch, but rather the kid who'd sat behind him in homeroom, or the one who traded notes with him in math class. Peripheral then and, now, irrelevant again.

But then Alex had shown up and something in him had felt a pull. It had been decades since he'd seen her, his high school girlfriend for half a second, a few frenzied gropes in dark bedrooms, a sense of dissatisfaction on both sides.

Still, there were moments that lingered, which was more than he could say for most people. He remembered one afternoon in Berkeley, not long after the accident, listening to *Emotional Rescue* in a sorority house where she was living for the summer. He was lying on a common room couch while she tinkled at a piano . . . or was that something he had read? No, don't do that, it was real enough: more real, even, for its echoes.

Of course, he and Alex had long since broken up by then, which only rendered the whole thing more affecting. For here was the thing—they had liked each other. Their brief interlude of dating had been a tunnel from which they had to emerge to become *friends*. Once she reappeared, all these years later, fuller of face and body but apparently the same, he kept thinking of these moments, hallmarks of an earlier incarnation, a different life, one he thought of now, when at all, with a bittersweet awareness of loss.

Alex was looking for something, that was certain, although he was relieved to understand that it was not romantic. No, it was something else, a quiet discontent obvious from her first message, which hinted at the usual middle-aged troubles: family complications, job dissatisfactions, the burden of raising teenage kids. *I'm a better parent from a distance*, she wrote about her older daughter, away at school now, the same age they had been when they'd last seen each other. He was reminded of Jonah, two years from college and counting every minute, by turns talkative and diffident, protective if not of the details then of the depths of his experience. Like son, like father, he realized.

When he wrote her back, he offered the merest summary of the personal— *married to Annie (for 20 years), two kids (Jonah, 17; Sadie, 13), been living in Los Angeles since 1991*—before shifting to work, and the trip, *this trip*, that he was planning to the Bay Area, where she still lived. They discussed details, traded messages like semaphores, like, what was that old cliché? *Ships in the night.* Yes, ships, he chuckled grimly, like the Titanic and the Carpathia. As he cycled through the Facebook messages, he kept imagining the past as a giant iceberg, ready to break him if he came too close. Maybe there *was* something to what he'd read. Maybe the past was a territory best left alone. But that was the challenge, wasn't it, of living at this moment? Anyway, if Alex was looking for something, he was, he realized, looking, also. When she suggested it, he didn't hesitate for half a second before agreeing to meet for a drink.

FOUR

Down in the Hole

Lately, he had been at a loss for words. Not in the sense of having nothing to add to the conversation, but in the sense of having nothing to say. He would find himself—at work, at home, in line for the movies—overwhelmed by something like pure feeling, except that it wasn't pure in any way he could put his finger on. There was no clarity, no direction, just a wave of . . . *distance* was the only way he could put it, as if he were in exile from his life. He would look around, struck by a sense of absolute isolation, unable to get outside himself. He had tried explaining this to Annie. But how could he describe the experience when he wasn't even sure what it felt like? Anything—a slant of light, the angle of a corner—could disconnect him, as if he had been cut adrift in the present with no reference points. Wherever he went, things looked familiar, but he was having trouble putting them together. He was, in other words, failing to make sense of it, even if he remained unsure of what exactly *it* was.

In any case, he didn't expect he'd say much, if anything, at the meeting. A little after four o'clock, he went downstairs and stepped into the stark January afternoon, light white, nearly transparent, shadows crisp and stark. It would be night when he got out. Even now, the afternoon was failing, sun low in the sky and a sharp breeze stirring, rustling the flags at the Mark Hopkins up the block. Where had the day gone? He had meant to get out this afternoon, to spend time in the city, but something had distracted him. Perhaps he was stalled by the image of all those people getting on and off the cable cars, the mechanistic nature of it, or perhaps the mechanistic nature of himself.

He remembered the first time he'd seen Nob Hill, riding the cable car up from the foot of California Street, hanging off the side and sticking his arms out, as if he were flying, free. Twenty-five years later, he'd done the same thing with Jonah, en route to the Fairmont's Laurel Court Bar. This was their tradition, to go to the Fairmont on the last evening they were in the city. Briefly he wondered if he'd end up there tonight. He smiled as he imagined Jonah, wandering the halls of the hotel as if he belonged, looking at the framed menus and the photographs. History for Jonah was still a story, exciting, exotic even. He wasn't old enough to feel the acceleration; he didn't realize yet that it was personal. What did it mean when all you knew was slippage, when even the people you loved were chimeras, when time kept sliding past you and there was nothing you could do? This was one of the reasons he'd wanted to reconnect with Alex, to pierce the veneer of the present, to take an axe to the frozen sea in him.

At the meeting, he sat at one end of a long conference table in a room overlooking the sparkle of the bay. In the distance, he could see the container port of Oakland, the Bay Bridge curving towards it like a question mark. From the start, he felt himself drifting. A woman laughed bitterly at the specter of an impending birthday. Another mentioned a friend who had just been diagnosed with stage three cervical cancer. Age and illness: the new vernacular. He listened half-heartedly, until he caught a glimpse of himself reflected in the window glass. So gray, he thought, unconsciously touching his hair, as if he were looking at one of those Facebook photos.

Was this who he he'd become, this middle-aged city planner, here to discuss transit hubs and the future of a city where he no longer lived? When had he gotten so sober, so responsible, so fluent in the little details by which we mark our lives? He wasn't in what he thought of as a mid-life crisis, not lamenting decisions, things he hadn't done. He loved his wife, his family, and yet he could see them shifting away from him. Tomorrow, Jonah would be leaving, when just yesterday he'd been as small as Sylvie's son. Sylvie, shit . . . and for a moment, he was arrested again by the memory of her and the boy in that backyard, beneath the hanging dagger of the sun.

FIVE

The Ninth Circle

It was dark when the meeting let out, and he found himself wandering aimlessly in the Financial District. The last hour and a half had been a blur, an emptiness, time discarded. He was glad to be outside, feeling the coolness of the evening, breeze sharp and static, buildings square against the sky. Almost without thinking, he walked to Montgomery Street, at the foot of the Pyramid, a crossroads in more ways than one. To his right, Columbus Avenue rose up through North Beach. To his left, the Russ Building, Market Street, the Palace Hotel. The Palace was where he'd agreed to meet Alex, in Maxfield's, with the Pied Piper mural above the bar. It wasn't a place he remembered from his time here. He hadn't discovered it until decades later, when he and Annie and the kids had stayed. They'd been back several times now, and he wondered whether it was why he'd suggested Maxfield's. Its layer of familiarity was a link to the present, a trail of crumbs to keep a place for him amidst the labyrinth of the past.

Alex had said 6:30. She had to be home for dinner. *Nobody around here can get a meal on the table*, she'd written, the grievance humorous or bitter, he couldn't tell. He took out his phone to check the time—6:15—and saw there was a text from Sadie, asking when he was coming home. At thirteen, she lived almost entirely in the future, short- *and* long-term, chattering about summer plans, what she wanted for her birthday, where she thought she wanted to go to college, all of it a limitless fantasy. It reminded him of something else he'd read, about the tension between kids and grown-ups. Our children were desperate to get us out of the way, because they understood that their true inheritance was the future, the one inheritance we could not withhold. He remembered feeling something similar, a longing for real life to begin. This was why he'd come to San Francisco, driving west with Jack as if it were a matter of destiny. On their first night in the city, in that studio on Haight Street, they had watched the darkness descend, lights snapping on like stars in the apartment buildings ringing Buena Vista Park. He had felt his body fill with breath as if, in leaving his past, his history, and coming here, he had been freed.

Now, of course, that *was* his past, a past so thick he felt encased. Standing here, he tallied echoes: the Pyramid, with its vaulted point and red eye at the apex, a vision of Atlantis, or so he'd once been told (and half-believed). The story had invested his time in San Francisco with a whisper of the mythological. This kind of magical thinking had led him also to Grace Cathedral, letting him imagine, briefly, that there was a shape, an order, to the world. The same was true of North Beach, although there, real history had left a residue: City Lights, the Condor, the hungry i. He knew better, knew that even landmarks had a habit of dissolving, that time was finite, and it always took its toll. No, this wasn't a midlife crisis, it was an *identity* crisis. Midway upon the journey of his life, within a shadowed forest where he had lost the straightforward path, he had the sense that there was more to it, that the issue was less dying than living, that there was something he hadn't learned yet, that same essential lesson: *be here now*.

The wind picked up, lashing him with bitter needles. He put his hands in his pockets and turned his collar up. Ahead, Montgomery Street unfolded to Market, the Palace growing visible in stages. First, the rounded corner of the building, yellow brick and cornices. Then, the marquee on the rooftop, spelling out its name in electric light. Another nod to the history of the city, to a different time. In one form or another, the Palace had stood on this corner since the 1870s, a vestige of that long-gone San Francisco, a phoenix risen from the ashes. The original had been destroyed in the 1906 earthquake, but the hotel was rebuilt three years later. It became an emblem of both San Francisco's substance and its insubstantiality, the way everything erected here could evaporate with the twitching of the fault.

He remembered pictures, downtown San Francisco after the quake and fire, streets scrubbed clean of buildings. The city in those images was little more than memory. Memory, yes, and also imagination, the vision of a city yet to come.

As an architect, he loved the mix of history and possibility, as if the form of the new city might be inscribed directly on the template of the old. There was also the filter of his own experience. He'd been through his first earthquake here, a medium-sized temblor late on an Easter Sunday afternoon. He could still recall the lurching, the ceiling fixture of his studio apartment swinging wildly, wood beams in the walls rat-tat-tatting out an SOS. It was hard to feel rooted, hard to see the permanence of anything you might construct in such an active landscape. Maybe that was part of his sense of the conditional, a physical reaction to living in California, on this elaborate peninsula, or in that sprawling megalopolis four hundred miles south.

He caught the light at Market, cutting in front of an F streetcar from Milan. A block west, he could see Lotta's Fountain, a legendary meeting place for survivors of the earthquake, dedicated in 1875 like the original Palace. A century later, there were no more survivors, and yet the fountain remained, a big bronze anchor jutting out from Market Street. He wondered where people would gather in the aftermath of the next quake.

One reason the 1906 earthquake was so *present* was the photographs. It had been the first disaster of the Kodak era, the first to be recorded by millions of informal snapshots. At the Cable Car Museum, on the other side of Nob Hill, you could still see the quake unfold on vintage stereopticons: streetscapes, rubble, women with bustle skirts and parasols. The entire city recorded its destruction with a willful cool. Like all photos, they promised a closeness they could not deliver. Here was a set of windows on a world that had disappeared in the very instant of its recreation. Time stopped and became solid, so close you felt you could step inside it, until you hit the surface of the frame. The same was true of his time in San Francisco, which was less about memory than memory suspended, like a solid shape he had both left behind and would never leave behind.

At the Palace, he glanced at his phone again—6:30, right on time. He passed through the lobby and down the corridor to Maxfield's, hearing the buzz of cocktail hour chatter, as familiar as the chirrups of tiny birds. By the door, he scanned the long mahogany bar, looking for a match to Alex's Facebook photo. Finally, he saw her, sitting with another woman at a table in the back. *Two women?* He had time to wonder in the second before she noticed him. Then Alex was waving and both women were standing and he was moving towards them. As he drew closer, confusion yielded to recognition which, in turn, became another layer of confusion. He identified first the faint smile and then the wary eyes of the other woman. Her features tumbled together like a succession of slides, familiar and yet at the same time, long-forgotten. Elena, his old high school girlfriend.

SIX

Interiors

His first thought was that he had been set up. He wasn't sure why, except for the look on Elena's face. He nodded self-consciously when Alex told him they'd been talking. Both lived in San Francisco, and they saw each other once a month, twice a month, for a drink or coffee. Elena had thought it would be fun to come along. Elena smiled then. She had little sharp predatory teeth, as white as fresh orange pith and as shiny as porcelain. The look she gave shook him, like a kind of earthquake, major or minor, it was too soon to tell. Large and small earthquakes began the same way, with a moment of rupture. The length of the fissure determined the severity of the shaking and the devastation that it caused. He could feel the rumbling as they said hello. *This was a mistake*, he thought, then pushed the idea away as he sat. A tiny flicker of something—unease? anxiety?—flared in his solar plexus like a flame.

Alex was effusive, Alex was excited, Alex was happy to see him. Her broad face broke into a smile. She chattered in a raspy voice, but he was having trouble making out the words. He ordered a drink, Jameson on the rocks, sipped greedily when it arrived. *I don't often drink hard liquor*, he found himself telling them . . . or did he only think it? Either way, he was too old for excuses.

And yet, just being here, just seeing Elena, made him feel like a high school kid again.

And what did that feel like? Tense, uncertain, self-conscious. As the alcohol seeped into him, he became aware of making small talk, as if he were watching himself in a play. He and Alex talked about high school, sharing stories of their children. Elena sat in the corner and watched them, flat half smile on her face. She was pretty, Elena was, prettier than in high school. Her hair was black and thick, expensively cut, shoulder length with bangs. He remembered her as raw-boned, blowsy, a big, fresh-faced girl he'd never bothered to get to know.

It had been unremarkable, their

relationship—or it would have been, if not for his virginity. Their first night together, she had taken off her clothes with an abandon that surprised him. Fumbling, over-eager, stunned at his good fortune, he had done the same. They hadn't gone very far, just rubbed against each other, but when they finally got dressed again and he walked her home, he knew he had crossed a border of some kind. Not crossed it—that would come later—but brushed right up against it. He was not thinking of sex but something equally exotic: the line separating childhood, adolescence, from the adult world.

Now, here they were, entrenched in that adult world, although adolescence kept pulling at him. Or maybe post-adolescence, that shadowy line again. He had teenagers. He knew from close observation just how young that was. Still, he also knew how the choices, the experiences, of that time continued to resonate. Wasn't that the point of this reunion? He was looking for something: roots, he guessed he would say. And yet, that was the problem with roots. They grew tangled and went in all sorts of unexpected directions, when you followed them back to the source.

Take Elena. She hadn't even been part of his San Francisco experience. Sure, she'd been around, a freshman at Berkeley when he and Jack landed in Haight-Ashbury. But after high school, she'd been wary. (*Be honest*, he told himself, *she wasn't the only one.*) It hadn't ended well between them, but ended in the only way it could. He blew her off after a series of graduation parties where he'd felt the need to say something, *to be consoling*, like the pressure of a noose. He'd been seventeen, the same age as Jonah, and he hadn't understood that she had feelings . . . or at least, feelings that were different from his. But that wasn't all of it, not exactly. It was that he *hadn't* had any real feelings that he'd wanted to keep.

On their last morning together, he had woken up at a friend's house. Fifteen or twenty kids huddled together in a basement rec room after a long and bleary night. Everyone was hungover, spaced from too much dope and drinking, edgy, raw with lack of sleep. He'd kept his distance, relieved that it was over and he wouldn't be seeing most of these kids again. Even then, he'd been a shedder, not the kind of person who liked to keep things, which made this whole weird day in San Francisco that much stranger, this three-dimensional gouging of the past.

But Elena hadn't let him off that easily. Elena hadn't let him walk away. She'd always had a toughness he couldn't penetrate—penetrate? Hell, that he couldn't *recognize*. He'd thought it was over when he left her in that basement. Now, in Maxfield's, he looked at the Pied Piper mural and wondered if time was a pied piper, leading him there to here. Elena was talking, and as her lips moved, he could feel his discomfort realign itself as the memory of desire. Elena had been his first . . . first fuck, first blowjob, first everything. She knew it and he knew it, and in the back of his mind, he couldn't help but wonder if that was why she was here. It wasn't like he'd had much experience subsequently. A couple of girlfriends and then he met Annie in college, and they'd been together ever since. *Was that part of this?* he asked himself, signaling for another drink.

So what are you doing in town? Elena asked, as if reading his mind, her voice pointed as a lance. He mentioned the meeting, talked for a moment about transit hubs, said he wasn't sure why he had made the trip. *Some things haven't changed, I guess*, she replied. Her bluntness stopped him. He squinted at her across the table, looking for a point-of-view. She was smiling again, mouth cracked open in a semblance of good nature, but her eyes were mica: flinty, fierce. *Why is she here?* he thought. *She doesn't like me.* And then, with a feeling a lot like that of vertigo, he realized that was precisely why she had come.

SEVEN

Barstool Blues

Later, he would wonder if he had mis-read things. Later, he would wonder if it was the alcohol. In the moment, though, he knew he was right. The realization struck with the force of revelation. He looked quickly towards Alex to see if she was aware. She seemed oblivious, sipping her Chardonnay, delighted to be out of the house even for an hour, to have a break before serving yet another meal. That was all she'd wanted, a quick flash of (re-)connection. As she sat there, her mouth unfolded lightly in a Cheshire cat grin. Alex, he remembered, had never been a talker. Even on that afternoon in

Berkeley, with "Emotional Rescue" blar-
ing from the speakers, she had been con-
tent to let the music talk for her. *You're
too deep in*, Mick Jagger had sung, *you
can't get out*. That was the danger of the
past, that it could rise up at any instant
and swamp you like the sea. And what
about the danger of the future, spar-
kling, offering promises it couldn't keep?
Again, the image of Sylvie rose before
him, so vivid it was almost as if she were
at the table with them, her body twisted
into a question mark. *No*, he thought,
and shook his head, rubbing his eyes to
mask the motion. He wondered how
long he needed to stay here. He wondered how he would get away.

Elena kept talking, but he wasn't
really paying attention—something

about her son, who was applying to law school, and her daughter, who was majoring in art. She hadn't spoken yet about her husband, but that didn't mean anything. She wasn't trying to show off. She wanted to put him in his place. She asked about his kids, nodded when he kept it general, telling her that they were teenagers. She knew how it was. Even as he mouthed the words, he was seized by a desire to protect them, not to reveal too much. It wasn't that they were under attack, but there was something dangerous about her tone, probing like a scalpel. *They must be interested in something*, she said, voice rising to a point. *They're kids*, he said, and laughed to shift the focus. He could not recall having dismissed them in such a way before.

Elena looked at him from across the table, her teeth flashing like little knives. *Kids?* she said. *We were kids too, back when we used to know each other. I'm not sure I know what you mean . . .* Her voice trailed off, a fading siren, and he felt as if he'd walked into a trap. Alex was sitting up now, closer to the table, rolling the stem of her wineglass in her hand. Her eyes were hooded, but he thought he saw a look of confusion there. *Help*, he wanted to say, but that seemed so dramatic, and in any case, help from what? When had it become risky to sit in a hotel bar with a couple of former friends and have a drink? And yet, he felt lost, as if this room had become a stage set and he was trapped within a play. *No*

Exit, he thought, or *Waiting for Godot*. I can't go on, I'll go on . . .

Elena was saying something else, her voice low but firm against the buzzing background of the bar. *Do you remember the last time we saw each other?* She leaned forward. *You don't, do you? I bet you don't.* He wanted to laugh at that, wanted to tell her how much he did remember. And yet, when it came to her, she wasn't wrong. He tried to recall when last he'd seen her. He knew it had been during his time in this city, but he couldn't bring the details to mind. *That's how little you mean to me*, he thought, reflecting again on their relationship, the way it had petered out with the school year, just another thing to leave behind.

He had never cared that much in the moment, certainly, and not after. He hadn't given her a second thought in all the years that divided them, as if she had disappeared.

For a second, he was aware of a breath of anticipation, as if Elena were expecting him to speak. Then the moment passed, and she turned to Alex, talking about people, just names really, none of whom he knew. He had the weird sense that this, too, was for his benefit, to show him how full her life had become. He was glad for her, although he understood that it had nothing to do with him. This was the irony. He had come to Maxfield's for one reason, and she, for another, and both were bound to leave here unfulfilled. Elena must have intuited this also. Eventually, she made a show of looking for the bar clock, and suggested that they get a check.

While they waited, Elena began describing an outdoor party she was planning. Her husband was turning fifty and she was catering a picnic at their house in the Berkeley Hills. *A catered picnic?* As she went on, he listened surreptitiously: a bar, a portable dance floor, heat lamps, and tables, each with a picnic basket as a centerpiece. *That's not a picnic*, he thought, but he knew better than to say anything. The check was coming, and he just wanted to get out. *The last time I went on a picnic* . . . and then it clicked, the memory swept over him.

It had been in Berkeley, deep in the spring, towards the end of the academic

year, late April, early May. She had
called him in San Francisco, stunning
since they hadn't seen each other in the
months since he'd arrived. There was
some event, he couldn't remember—a
concert? a performance?—and she'd suggested a picnic first. After picking him
up at the downtown Berkeley BART
station, she drove him in her little car
to Strawberry Canyon, a spot overlooking Memorial Stadium. She'd spread out
a blanket and served fried chicken and
California Chablis. Then, once he was
full, stretched out beneath the blood red
Berkeley sunset, she had lit into him,
telling him how much he had hurt her,
voice low but insistent, her words as
sharp as little blades.

Sitting in Maxfield's, he could feel

his insides churning, as if the bottom of his stomach had fallen out. It was all so close, telescoped into an instant, with her right before him, and also inaccessible, in the past. He kept a neutral look on his face—the payoff of all those years of meetings—but behind the wall of his eyes he was scrambling, his mind a pair of ragged claws scuttling across the floors of silent seas. What else had she said? He couldn't quite bring it back, but he could sense the flavor of it, knew that it had to do with how much she had cared for him, how she had felt betrayed.

At another time, in another moment, he might have dismissed this as fantasy. How could something that had happened so long ago, something that had never seemed important, continue to haunt her? Then again, just look at him. Wandering the city as if it were a ghost town, walking the Stations of the Cross. Occasionally, Annie would talk about the boys she'd known in college, or someone she'd dated briefly before she had met him. *He was hard to get rid of,* she had said of one such former paramour just a few nights ago, riding in the car with him and Jonah. Although he'd laughed and told her to get over herself, he wasn't laughing now.

Thinking about that night, he found himself all of a sudden imagining Elena at eighteen. The veil of her sophistication had slipped, leaving that slightly horsy, awkward girl behind. He could see her, see her impression of a smile, lips tight, uncertain, as if the worst sin would be to laugh. Was this what had attracted him, that diffidence, that shyness? He couldn't remember, and besides it didn't matter anyway. For when he saw her as eighteen, it wasn't from the point-of-view of his younger self, but more like a parent. He knew so many girls like this—*his own daughter*—and he knew how deep their feelings ran. No wonder Elena was still nursing . . . whatever it was, a grudge, a sliver of resentment. No wonder the memory had lingered and she had shown up here to see it through.

He took a last sip of whiskey, now mostly water from the melted ice. He set the glass on the table precisely, matching its edges to the damp impression on the cocktail napkin, as if getting them to sync up was the most important thing in the world. No one was saying anything. Silence sat like a balloon between them, a balloon they were afraid to pop. *I . . .* , he started, but then he let the syllable trail off, like an error or an afterthought. It was a symbol of all he should say and all that he would never say, an apology he would never make.

When the check came, he reached for it and, waving off their protestations, gave the waiter his credit card. It seemed both expected and utterly insufficient, a gesture, like all the others, destined to fall short. Elena was watching him, but he was afraid to look at her, afraid it might trigger something, afraid of what he might say. *I'm sorry?* But what good would that do? It had all happened so long ago, and anyway, who knew what she was thinking? It would only make things worse.

And so, he sat there, waiting, face blank, at a loss for words. He signed the slip and got up, watched as they both stood in turn. They hugged. A loose embrace with Alex, a stiff clench with Elena. *So much to be said*, he thought, *so much that will never be said.* Then he turned and left the bar.

EIGHT

Ulysses in Nighttown

Market Street was a relief, crowded, clanging, the sky above compressed but open: full dark, no stars. For the first time in an hour, he felt like he could breathe. He meandered up the block, crossed the street and stopped at Lotta's Fountain. Like a survivor, which was what he was, of course . . . for the time being, anyway. Around him, the city continued its relentless motion—street-cars, tourists, commuters, hustlers, a cacophony of speed and light. And yet, here he was, at the center of it, at the *epi*center, totally unnoticed. He took solace in his anonymity.

After a moment, he went right on Kearny Street and started north. He was not walking towards anything so much as away from everything. His goal was to get lost in the city, to pursue a trail that could not be traced. He turned on Sutter, and again on Grant, following the broad sidewalk to the Chinatown gate. On the other side, the street was like a carnival, a crazy quilt of signs and sound and movement, as garish as a sequence from a film. The sidewalks were full of people drifting, talking, looking up at the pagoda roofs of the buildings, taking photographs. California Street was two blocks ahead, but he couldn't bring himself to take the plunge. Instead, he turned on Bush and cut over to California on Stockton, where, muscles in both calves burning, he began to climb Nob Hill.

The idea was to return to the hotel, order room service, hide out until it was time to go home. Maybe later he would go to the Laurel Court, lift a glass to Jonah, to the present, to all he had left to do. Memory was a trap. He had always known it. It could eat you if you let it. Just look at his encounter with Elena. *Elena*, he thought, her face rising before him, half as she had once been and half as she was now. He began to understand, as he crossed first Powell and then Mason Street, that his was a peculiar kind of memory, defined by landscape, even his own inner landscape, but at the same time—and with few exceptions—curiously devoid of humanity.

The realization stopped him on the sloping sidewalk, with the Mark Hopkins glowering above him, a dark shape against the sky. It was true, he knew as soon as he thought it, and in that instant he felt more alone than he had all day. What use was his connection to these streets, to the vista of this skyline, what good his memories of this place? All it had left him with were pictures, intercut with a few small film clips: Alex in the sorority house, that Sunday service at Grace Cathedral. His memory was like a Facebook page, a set of scattered images, posted as if they meant something when they revealed nothing at all. Generic, he scoffed, or worse, empty. And that was the whole problem, wasn't it, that he was an empty vessel, that his disengagement was not a function of getting older but had been a part of him all along.

He pinched his eyes as if to squeeze the thought out, pushed up the hill towards his hotel. But half a block shy, he veered, almost instinctively, across the street. The last thing he wanted was to be alone in a room, trapped like a hamster on a wheel. No, that was just another sinkhole. He needed more stable ground. So he kept on, past the Pacific-Union Club, past Grace Cathedral and down California towards Van Ness, sidewalk sparsely dotted with pedestrians, lights on in the low-slung buildings, small and sketchy in the night.

He could feel his body fall into a groove now, legs pumping like a machine.

He could feel his heart achieve a steady rhythm, feel the flow of his own blood. It was a sensation he knew well: the oblivion of the long-distance walker, moving street to street, neighborhood to neighborhood, passing along the outer edges of a million lives. Like a ghost, he thought, drifting down the sidewalks, looking into the lit-up windows, watching all those solitary men and women as they went about their routines. Solitary, yes, even when they were together, faces staring at each other across the dinner table, eyes hooded, mouths working in a quiet mumble as they tried to find something to say. How many times had he felt the same?

He turned right at Van Ness, followed it to Lombard, went up to Fillmore and cut over towards Marina Green. He had worked here, all those many years ago, canvassing for Greenpeace out of an office in Fort Mason. Most nights, after going door to door in Berkeley, in Albany, in Daly City, he had waited for the bus at Fillmore and Chestnut, or taken the long walk back to the Haight across the darkened city. Fillmore through Pacific Heights and then up Clay or Sacramento to Divisidero, watching the neighborhoods change, chic to shabby, feeling the pulse of the streets rise up inside him like some kind of umbilical connection. He had walked, then, in a kind of fugue state of exhilaration. But tonight, as he pushed himself, first towards the water and then east, up the hill and past the

Black Point Battery, it was exhaustion he sought.

He remembered, a decade ago, the first time he had taken Jonah here, showing him the cannons and the secret staircase (not so secret, although he had always thought of it as his alone). It had been overgrown then, and remained so now. As he started down, a shadow in the silent evening, he felt a brief glimmer of . . . resolution? No, nothing that complete. Yes, he had passed his love of San Francisco on to Jonah. Yes, it had become a bond they shared. And yet, what if it was all a frozen landscape, past and present blurred together? *He was barely here, he had never been more than barely here.* He came back into the grid at Beach Street and slid along the front of Ghirardelli Square. All the lights and tourists, the street musicians and the clatter of the cable cars, even on a cool evening in November, only made it worse by reminding him of his disconnection, as if not just his life but everyone's had passed him by.

The crowds were dense, the crowds were pressing, the crowds were a bubbling current that threatened to sweep him away. There was too much noise, too many flashing signs. It was the landscape of a nightmare come to life. He felt his stomach fall again, a queasy sensation like being on a roller coaster, nauseous with the idea that he did not exist at all. Eyes down, concentrating on his breathing, he skirted the tumult until he got to Columbus, where he headed into North Beach. Then, he turned right on Taylor Street and began the slow, slogging climb in the direction of his hotel.

NINE

Labyrinth

But a funny thing happened on the way to the hotel. He found himself redeemed. Or not redeemed so much as confused, beguiled . . . or maybe it was seduced, again, by the pull of the city and its interplay between the present and the past. He was breathing hard as he reached Clay Street, legs heavy, lower back starting to tug at him in an intimation of middle age. Over his shoulder, San Francisco opened in a sea of lights. Up ahead, all he could see was Grace Cathedral, and, just beyond it, the slender tower of his hotel.

He paused, panting, fingers splayed

across his thighs. Then he took one step, and another, his point of view shifting the higher he went. The Cathedral seemed to rise out of the hilltop, its double tower like an outstretched hand. It was not magical, he understood now, but supplicating, a prayer in concrete to the empty universe, a declaration of both desperation and desire. Desire? Yes, the desire to be noticed, the desire to leave a mark. *Here we be*, the building seemed to be exclaiming, *not for long, but here we be.* You could keep on moving, or you could roll up and die. The second option was assured, sooner or later, which meant that the only decision of any consequence was what you did about the first.

Across Sacramento, the steps of the

Cathedral beckoned. He took out his phone to check the time. 9:30, after his long peregrination through the city, and not a single message. In every way that mattered, he was on his own. He thought about calling Annie, texting the kids. But they were in their lives, four hundred miles to the south of him. He was not part of them, not tonight.

And yet, those steps. They shone white beneath the streetlights, leading to the Cathedral's double door. He followed them up, first one level, then a second, until he was on a little flat plain of plaza, with the rectory off to his right. Just to the east, tucked into an open-air rotunda, he could see the outline of a labyrinth, a model of the maze inlaid in the Cathedral, which was itself a replica of the labyrinth at Chartres. He knew a little about labyrinths, having walked one once on a bluff overlooking the Pacific Ocean at Santa Cruz. The original labyrinths—or the original Christian labyrinths—had been built as *chemins de Jerusalem*, landscapes for a proxy pilgrimage. But the goal, especially in California, had long since shifted to personal discovery. He recalled walking the narrow lines in the failing sunlight, mist blurring the edges of the ocean, rendering it in shades of bluish white. He had been skeptical—he was always skeptical. But as he had followed the looping lanes of the maze, focused on staying within the boundaries, his sense of both past and future had receded. He was left in time and yet outside it, mind and body finally still. He had never told anyone about that, not even Annie. It had seemed too . . . too personal, too intimate to share. Now, however, he remembered the way that calm had descended upon him about halfway through his silent passage. Without thinking, he moved slowly towards the mouth of *this* labyrinth, and embarked upon its winding path.

For an instant, he grew self-conscious. There was no one here, but he knew he could be seen from the windows of the adjacent hotels and apartments. He felt a twinge, a shudder, at the thought of people looking at him. Then he remembered Sylvie, and how he'd watched *her* through that kitchen window, watched her pushing her son on the swing as if the world had shrunk to the two of them. Sylvie hadn't cared. She was consumed by the moment. She understood that the moment was all there was. He wanted some of that same understanding. It was all he wanted, a way to fend off his fear and longing—or not fend off, but a way to integrate them instead.

He took a step, and another. The labyrinth was divided into quarters. The idea was to walk each section in succession until you made it to the middle, and after that, to walk your way back out again. In Santa Cruz, it had taken hours, but this labyrinth seemed smaller. Anyway, where did he have to be? He thought about Elena, about Alex. He thought about Annie and the kids. He thought about Sylvie, fighting the good fight, even though it was a fight that she—that no one—could win. He thought about himself here, alone, adrift, so little to hold onto, as it was and as it would ever be. Then, he placed one foot before the other, perspective narrowing to the path in front of him, mind a blank except for one thought, a simple benediction, which he repeated, to the rhythm of his walking. *Be here now.*